THOMAS B. TURTLE

THOMAS B. TURTLE

Lisa Brooks

Illustrations by
Augusta Talbot

Exposition Press ⊗ Hicksville, New York

*To Ollie and the children
and to my brother Allan*

Contents

THOMAS B. TURTLE

Tom Turtle
Finds a Life

The pond lay in front of them. It was wiggling with tadpoles. Clumps of frogs' eggs hung like clouds in a sky of water. They had reached their flight of fancy.

He sat in there somewhere. They were after him—the big green slippery frog.

"Me first!" said Barnes. "I'm the girl." She raised her hand and held up four fingers. "I'm this many and I see gooder!"

"Me next!" shouted Oliver. He put up his hand, trying to pull down his thumb and little finger to hold the three fingers in between up straight. "I amma policeman."

Allan held his hand up too. He couldn't count. It didn't matter. He was only two and always last. He followed behind Oliver, tripped and fell. "I all wet."

"Croak—Garrump."

"It's him, walk slow. Don't scare 'im up," ordered Barnes. They circled the pond slowly—a lion, followed by a tiger, followed by an alligator, stalking their prey—the big green slippery frog.

"Pop-ker-plunk."

"He got away," screamed Barnes, upset. Happy-go-lucky Oliver pulled up his bathing suit, swam into the deepest part of the pond, and grabbed the big green slippery frog by its back legs. He swam back to shore and handed the frog to Barnes.

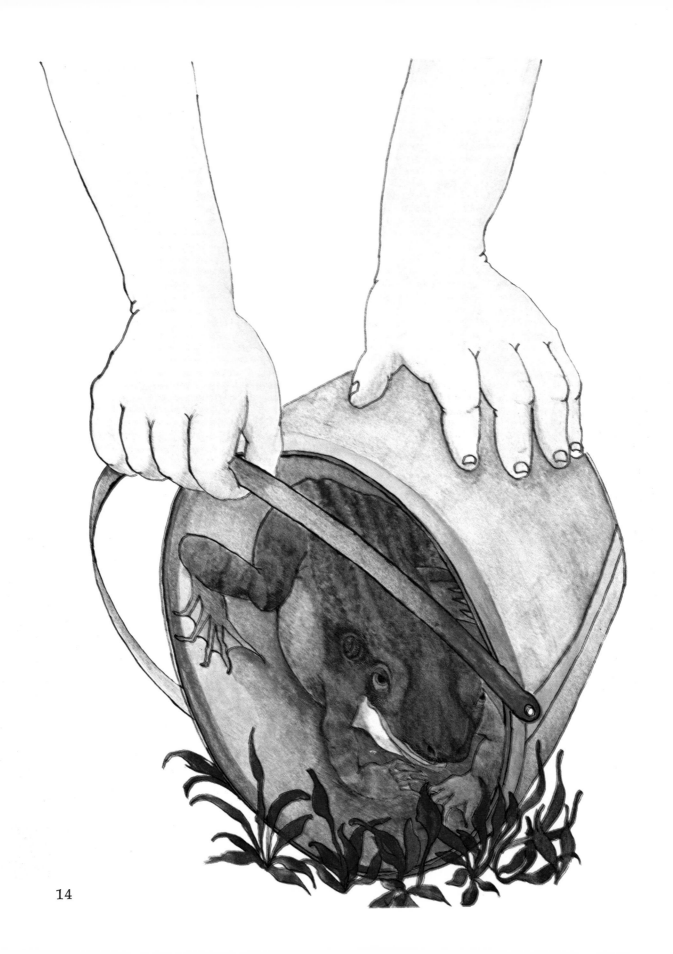

"We got 'im, Oliver! We got 'im!" shouted a very excited Barnes. He filled the whole pail.

Allan crouched over it. "Look at 'im. He gots feets like us!"

"Watch him, Allan," ordered Barnes, who returned to the pond with her net. "Hey, Oliver, come quick! I got a tadpole with feets growing out the back!"

"I got somethin' too, Barnes."

Allan rustled over to Oliver. "Let me see, Olverr." Oliver threw it with all his might into the pond. Allan screamed.

"Look, Allan," said Oliver. "It floats. It's a boat and all the people on it are going to drown." Allan watched the hump in the water paddle across to the other side, where Barnes arrived at a dead gallop and picked the hump out of the pond.

"It's just a dumb rock." Barnes liked it though and felt the bulge in her pocket to make sure it was there. Then she hurried back to the pail. "Allan, where's the frog? You lost him!"

Allan looked into his empty hands, "Somewheere."

She looked into the pail, trying to catch the frog with her eyes and put him back where she had seen him last.

Oliver, the policeman, tricycled home in his police car, talking into his walkie-talkie hand. Allan, a fire truck, sirened home between sniffles. Barnes galloped home, a wild pony. She took a stick and slapped herself to make the pony in her go faster.

At home, Barnes dumped out her pockets. There was the pretty mica rock that shined. Oh, the brown oak leaf was crackled and broken. The two acorns had lost their hats and were no good.

"Come here, Oliver," Barnes said. "Come quick." Allan toddled over to Barnes from the corner, his thumb in his mouth. Oliver saw Allan go and rushed over too. They huddled around Barnes to look. In her hand was the rock from the pond.

"It moved! I felt it move!" Barnes exclaimed.

Oliver grabbed Barnes's hand. "I found it; it's mine."

"No, mine," said Allan from habit.

"It's we're's; we'll share it, OK?" said Barnes. Barnes opened her hand.

They watched the rock as two pebbles came out of each side. A tiny worm twisted out of one end of the rock. Out of the other end, a green bulge slowly emerged. Out of the bulge, two eyes opened up and looked at them as they watched.

"It's a moo-cow," screeched Allan.

"No, Allan," corrected Oliver. "It's a truck; it's got wheels."

"Hi, I'm Tom Turtle," it said.

"I told you so," said Barnes. "It's a turtle. It just said so."

"No, I'm Tom Turtle," he replied.

Tom Turtle Finds a Home

Barnes stashed Tom in her pocket. He poked his head out. "Please, oh please. It's dark in here. The worms wiggle and frighten me. The gravel gets in my mouth."

"We'll build you a real house then," decided Barnes.

Oliver rushed out to the workshop. There were the big shiny work tools. They made Oliver very happy. The hammer went bang, bang, bang against the wall. The screwdriver jabbed into the dirt floor and twisted around. The saw sawed until its teeth got stuck in the workbench. The box of nails opened all by itself and spilled out on the floor. Then Oliver grabbed all the tools in his arms and dropped them in the driveway, where he sat down beside them.

Allan ran out to the sandpile. His backhoe dug out a big hole. His dump truck carried the sand away. His dump truck brought the sand back and dumped it in the hole. His bulldozer packed it down. Then Allan took his cement mixer and ran it back and forth, crashing it against the fence until he fell over on top of it.

Barnes took to the garden, taking Tom with her to make sure he didn't get lost. She pulled out clumps of pretty flowers by the roots, leaving black holes in the garden bed. "You can't have roses; they have thorns and you'd get prickled. Violets and daffodils are very pretty, don't you think?" Tom soaked his outstretched head in the sun and watched Barnes talk. He didn't know much about flowers.

Tom spent the night in an old, baby's bathtub in the barn. He spent many nights in the barn in the baby's bathtub. "Oh please, oh please," he begged them. "The horses snort and stomp their feet at night. They scare me."

"Maybe he wants to take a walk," suggested Barnes.

"He's funny," said Oliver.

"I like ketchup on my hamburger. He nice froggie," commented Allan.

Out on the grass, Tom crawled very hard. They followed him on their hands and knees. Something inside Tom was telling him where to go. He went up the road. They went after him. Then Tom stopped.

"What are we doing here?" asked Barnes. "We're at the pond! You like it here? You want to live here?" Barnes didn't understand.

"I like it here," said Tom.

"Well, I've got to get my trucks," said Oliver, excited.

Barnes started to pack a castle out of mud. She pushed pretty stones into the castle until it was tall and round. She used pieces of broken glass, from the glass Allan threw on the floor at lunch, to make windows. She tore off a piece of bark for a door. She found a soft fuzzy leaf for his bed. She planted the garden flowers all around his house. "There!" she sighed at last, very pleased with her work.

Oliver arrived with a barrage of trucks. His mouth foamed and the motors of the trucks rolled out roads, got stuck in the mud, and crashed against the trees. He nearly took the pond apart and ran highways all around and into it. He did a good job.

In the meantime, Allan squeezed Tom in his hand while he sat.

"Allan, don't squeeze so hard," yelled Barnes. Allan sneered. Tom didn't mind. He had tucked his head and feet and tail into his shell to take a nap.

"All done!" screamed Barnes.

"Me, too," said Oliver, tired of his trucks.

Tom awoke and looked at his new home. He couldn't believe his eyes. "It's beautiful!"

"Yes," said Barnes. "It's time to go home."

"I gotta go home, Barnes," said Oliver, holding his pants. It was getting dark anyhow.

Tom heard the trucks roar down the road toward the farm. He heard Allan scream as Oliver crashed into him. He heard Barnes screech like a pony.

"Let's race home, Oliver. Come on!"

Then there was no more noise. Tom stood outside the bark door of his beautiful mud-and-stone castle, beside the idyllic pond. Suddenly, Tom felt very lonely.

Tom Turtle
Finds His Friends

Next morning, something inside Tom made him crawl away from the pond, away from his palace, down the road toward the farm. He crawled along the post-and-rail fence. Would the fence end? Would it go on forever with him alongside of it? Would he ever find his friends again?

Tom could almost feel Oliver's hand around him. It was always hot and sweaty. It was gooey with jelly, but it was so warm. Barnes's hand was slightly cold, but clean and careful—always gentle. Allan's hand was the perfect size. Tom fit in just right, but Allan squeezed so hard Tom worried he would get squished right out of his shell. "What would I be like then?" Tom felt them hold him one by one. "Oh, I hope they don't drop me." Tom crawled harder.

Then there was a post, but no rails, and Tom looked down a long road. He saw a gray house. "They're there." He saw a white house. "No, they're there." He saw a brown house. "They're there; they must be." Then he saw a red house. "Where are they?"

He crawled down the road. A black-and-white furry animal ran circles around him yapping. Then two lime green eyes caught him. A leg, stretched out like a fork, poked at him and turned him over. Then the barking dog chased the green cat eyes away.

Tom was at the brown house. He crawled in. Suddenly, above him was a rumbling roof, and, around him, balls spinned and threw dirt in his face. The tractor and wagon backed out of the garage. They didn't live here.

29

Tom crawled to the gray house and under the door. A bunch of black feathered animals rushed over to him and started pecking him on the shell. Tom crawled out. They didn't live here. This was the chicken house.

Tom crawled toward the red house. He passed a pen. Three bare-naked animals stuck their snouts through the wire and sniffed at him. Tom quickly crawled past the pigs. Then there was more fence. Tom heard funny loud noises. They followed him along the fence.

Moo—Moo—Moo. Tom was scared. Tom crawled up the ramp into the red house. It looked familiar. The floor shook. Tom looked up. He was under a big brown horse and the horse was pawing the floor. He was going to get stepped on. Then the swish of a tail knocked Tom and his whole shell tossed and turned. Tom landed in a bale of hay. Tom remembered where he was now. "They don't live here —no, not in the barn." Tom wasn't going to find them—not anywhere —not ever again.

Suddenly, hay fell on top of Tom's head.

"Hey, Tom." He heard their voices. No, he was imagining it.

"Hey, Tom, up here."

Where were they? Tom stretched his neck out and around. He didn't see them. More hay fell down on his head.

"Scared you, huh?" laughed Barnes. "Look, we're up here in the hayloft." Tom looked up. "Sorry we scared you." Tom wasn't scared anymore at all. He'd never been so happy in all his life.

Tom Turtle
and Truman

"Who's he?" asked Tom.

"He's Truman; he's a baby," answered Barnes.

"Well, where'd he come from?" demanded Tom.

"Out of Mommy's tummy. We all hatched like that. We're all Brookses."

Tom looked sad. He didn't know where he'd come from. But Barnes, Oliver, and Allan were his friends. They liked him. He liked them.

"What's a baby doing with us?" asked Tom.

"Well, we have to have him. He belongs to us. He came home one day, like you did, but he's we're's."

Tom looked hurt.

"He's going to walk by himself pretty soon," said Oliver proudly. He lifted Truman up in his arms and carried him toward Tom. Truman laughed out loud when Oliver's arms lifted him up. "Come on, little truck. Show Tom how you walk. Come on, little battle tractor. He's getting heavy, Barnes," said Oliver, panting. Truman thudded onto the ground and began to cry. Oliver rolled Truman over and tickled him on the tummy. Truman giggled and laughed. "He likes that."

Allan came over and sat on Truman's tummy. Truman laughed again.

"Well, I tickle too. It's easy," said Tom. "Oliver, come here," pleaded Tom. "Scratch my tummy. I'll show you; I laugh hard, harder than that."

But Truman was laughing so hard nobody could hear Tom talking. Barnes, Oliver, and Allan crowded around Truman. His giggling ended up making them all laugh, all except Tom.

Then Allan bit Truman on the foot. Truman screamed.

"Come on, little tractor," said Oliver. "It's OK." Oliver pulled his hair. Truman screamed louder.

"I hate that noise," Barnes stomped her feet. "He makes me angry when he cries."

"I don't like him either," agreed Tom. Barnes, Oliver, and Allan didn't hear Tom. Truman was crying too hard.

Tom crawled closer to Barnes, Oliver, and Allan. "I've got to make them tickle me. They'll see how good I tickle!"

Suddenly, Truman stopped crying. His eyes followed the moving thing. He started to giggle. He raised himself up on his knees and hands and crawled after Tom. Tom crawled as fast as he could away from Truman.

"Hey, let's have a race," suggested Barnes. They put Tom and Truman side by side. "On your mark, get set, GO!" This was the crawl of Tom's life. He crawled hard, as hard as he could.

"That baby is a big bad wolf. He's a hungry red fox," Tom kept telling himself. "He's a fire-breathing dragon and he'll burn me up." Tom crawled faster and faster. He heard the delighted giggle following right behind him. It giggled and gained on him. It was catching up. He felt a hand, smaller than usual, grab him, hold him up, drop him. He crawled harder. The little hand got Tom again, stuffed him in its slobbery mouth and clamped down. Tom felt a little tooth dent into his shell.

Then Oliver took Tom out of Truman's mouth. "That's not good for you. No, no, Truman. You could choke and suffocate." But Truman had won the race.

"He bit me!" cried Tom.

"See, Tom, he has a tooth. Look, a real tooth, and he's going to get more," said Oliver.

"It hurt me," said Tom.

Oliver, Allan, and Barnes were very proud of Truman. He won the race. He had a tooth in his mouth. He was going to walk.

Tom looked at Truman. "He's disgusting. He disgusts me. He can't walk. He cries. He bites. He can't talk. I wouldn't want one of those."

Then Truman started to cry again. He screamed. He got red in the face. Nothing worked. Barnes talked to him. "STOP IT!" He didn't pay any attention. Oliver turned him over to tickle him. He cried louder.

Tom Turtle crawled over to Oliver. He'd show them how good he tickled. Not like that yelling baby. Truman's eyes saw Tom crawl. Truman smiled at Tom. Tom looked back at him. Truman started to crawl after Tom. He laughed and giggled out loud.

"Hey, Tom, he likes you. He does. Look, he likes you. You're a Brooks!"

"He does?" said Tom. "He likes me? I'm a Brooks too, like you?" So Tom crawled hard with Truman chasing him. It wasn't so bad this time. Barnes, Oliver, and Allan laughed. Truman laughed. Tom laughed.

"Hey, Tom, you can stop. Truman is asleep," observed Barnes.

"Yeah, now we can go play," said Oliver eagerly, as all three Brookses started to run.

Tom watched them, torn with indecision. Should he go and play with his old friends, or should he stay and take care of his new one? Slowly Tom Brooks Turtle crawled onto Truman's tummy. Truman giggled rapturously.

Tom Turtle
and Me-Pony

Barnes and Tom straddled the post-and-rail fence looking at Me-Pony. Me-Pony was the special black-and-white spotted pony—black African-panther black, and white Easter-rabbit white. Barnes was "me," and the pony was hers.

"She's beautiful, Barnes," wooed Tom. Me-Pony was nuzzling against Barnes's face and rubbing at her boot.

"Well, just watch this," Barnes clapped her hands. Me-Pony threw up her head. Her tail sprang up. She snorted and pranced around in circles, picking her feet up high. "Clap-clap." Me-Pony, startled, kicked her back legs out at the blue sky. Then she began to gallop, so fast you couldn't separate her feet, and her mane and tail waved like branches in the strong wind—so fast she flew past the fence, above the green grass, through the blue sky, and out of sight. Barnes flew after her. Then Me-Pony galloped back around and screeched to a halt in front of Tom. Barnes was there too, beside him.

"She's frisky, huh, Barnes," said Tom. Suddenly, Me-Pony fell to the ground. "Is she all right?" asked Tom.

"Sure, just watch," assured Barnes.

Me-Pony kicked her legs up in the air again and again until her fat body rolled over.

"She did a somersault just right!" exclaimed Tom. "But look, Barnes, her white spots are all dirty now. Barnes . . . Barnes . . . ?"

But Barnes wasn't listening. She was watching her beautiful pony prance. Her eyes sparkled.

"Barnes!"

"Oh, don't worry, Tom. The rain will wash her off."

Me-Pony stood up and shook. Dust filled the air. She snorted and smoke came out of her nostrils. Tom was scared. Me-Pony walked over to Barnes and nuzzled against her face.

"Tom, go get me some carrots."

"I will," said Tom gladly. He crawled fast toward the house.

Tom brought out a bag of carrots along with Oliver and Allan. Tom looked into the pasture. Barnes was galloping up and down. She whinnied. She threw her head. She rolled over on the ground. She jumped over a branch. Tom looked puzzled. Was it Barnes or Me-Pony? Barnes galloped over to Tom and took a bite of carrot with her mouth. "She's beautiful," wooed Tom. Barnes whinnied a "yes."

"I want a turn on that pony there, Barnes," screamed Oliver, chewing a carrot and looking at his bucking bronco.

"I'll go saddle her up," said Barnes.

Me-Pony, with a bridle in her mouth and a saddle on her back, stood ready. Oliver's cowboy hat covered his whole face up, and his boots were so twisted out of shape, he tripped.

"Watch me get up," said Oliver to Tom. Barnes hoisted him up and he sat there. "Gitty-up." Me-Pony stood still, disinterested. "Watch me get down," said Oliver. Oliver slipped over one side and fell down under Me-Pony's legs. Me-Pony stood still like a statue. Oliver's cowboy hat fell off his head. He grabbed it and climbed up on the fence. He situated his hat right on his head and punched it on.

"Want a turn?" Barnes asked Allan.

Allan scrambled to the other side of the fence where he was safe. He chewed on a carrot and spat it out. "Donna want to."

"Well, I'm taking her up the road," said Barnes, "on a trail ride, a real trail ride through the woods." Up she climbed, and Me-Pony trotted off with Barnes astride. As they trotted up the road steadfastly together, Oliver and Allan went to the sandpile and trucks.

Tom sat alone on the top rail of the fence. The top rail of the fence made a good pony for Tom—another Me-Pony.

"I'm going riding too, on you—a real trail ride." Tom bounced up and down on the fence, trotting. "She's frisky today," said Tom. He was posting. Up the road, on the Fence-Pony after Barnes—under the hickory-nut tree. Nuts fell on top of Fence-Pony and Tom. Fence-Pony shied. Tom fell to one side. "That's all right, girl," said Tom.

A stick curled upon the road, uncurled and slithered away. "A snake!" Tom leaned down and covered up Fence-Pony's eyes. "Glad you didn't see that, girl." Then a big truck zoomed around the corner past the fence. "It could have crashed into us, girl," said Tom. Then Tom lost his balance. Fence-Pony jumped and bucked and threw him off. "The big bad wolf chased us, but he didn't get us, girl, and you got us home safe and sound."

Tom crawled down to the barn. His shell ached from his fall. He waited there for Me-Pony and Barnes to get back from their trail ride. He held what was left of the bag of carrots. He took one out and started to chew on it.

Tom Turtle
and the
Pussy Willows

"They're fuzzy and gray and alive. They're mice. I know it."

"They aren't, Tom; they're pussy willows. They're soft and gray, but they aren't animals—they're buds. Underneath are green leaves," explained Barnes.

"They're joking you," said Tom. "They're mice. I'm going to put out a pan of water and a pan of grain, and you'll see. They'll climb down from that branch and eat and drink it up. You watch."

So they put the dish of water and pan of grain underneath the bush and left it there until the next day.

The next day, they came back and looked in the dish and pan.

"See, I told you, Tom."

Tom looked; the dish was full of water and the pan was full of grain. "That's funny," said Tom. "I was sure. They're so fuzzy and gray and warm. They must be mice. They must be."

"Well," said Barnes, throwing up her hands, "you don't understand. You don't understand! I'm cutting down a bunch of pussy willows and putting them in the vase in the house. They'll look pretty in the house."

They carried the branches home, and the gray soft pussy willows, the first flowers in the house, looked friendly and warm in the vase.

"Don't they look pretty?" said Barnes, admiring her work.

"Yes, they do," agreed Oliver, not looking.

Allan picked off a fuzzy one. Then he screamed, "It bit me; it bit me!" and threw the gray pussy willow on the floor. Barnes rushed over and slapped Allan hard on his back.

"Don't do that, Allan; you're ruining the flowers. Stop it!"

Allan whimpered, "It bit me."

"Oh, shush."

"Isn't he silly?" commented Oliver.

"He's a bad boy," corrected Barnes.

That night Barnes dreamt about pussy willows changing into mice.

The next morning, Barnes ate breakfast. She looked at the vase. The pussy willows were gone, and stark branches stared Barnes in the eyes. "My pussy willows—Allan?"

Allan looked at Barnes. "No, didn't."

"Allan?"

"No, didn't."

Barnes slapped Allan hard on the back. "Don't do that ever again!"

Barnes went out and chopped the pussy willow bush down, bringing in an overpowering vaseful of new soft furry pussy willows. "Aren't they beautiful?"

The next morning, Oliver went into the breadbox to get some bread to toast. There were holes in the bread and Oliver couldn't find a single whole perfect piece of bread, which made him jump up and down, rip the loaf of bread to shreds, throw them on the floor, and fall down crying. "Get me some more."

"Oh, go get a banana, Oliver. There's one with a tag on it," assuaged Barnes.

Oliver got the banana with the tag on it, but in the middle of the banana was an enormous hole. "Ruined!" screamed Oliver. "Barnes, all the pussy willows are gone again—all of them, look!"

"Allan?" screamed Barnes. Then Barnes saw a pussy willow run across the floor into a corner hole in the wall. She looked in the breadbox and saw four pussy willows scramble out the back, behind the breadbox, into the wall. She pulled a pillow off the couch and saw twenty-four pussy willows huddled in a corner, jump off the couch, and disappear into cracks in the floor.

52

Tom stopped by that morning.

"They're smart pussy willows," he said.

"What do we do about them now?" asked Barnes.

"You set traps for them all over the house, catch them, and throw them out," said Tom.

They set the traps and each time they heard a snap, another pussy willow was caught, and the traps snapped all day and night, 'til the pussy willows were all caught.

Outdoors, all the bushes were now covered with pussy willows. Barnes knew the fattest ones were the ones she had let indoors. She looked at them in amazement. No matter how much she petted them, they never moved or opened their eyes.

Tom Turtle
and the Tree

Tom had always wanted to climb trees. Everyone could except him. Barnes waved to him from up in the tippy-top of the tree. "Hello, down there."

Oliver, halfway up the tree, didn't go farther, but he looked down at Tom. "Can't get me; try to reach me."

Even Allan could climb up and sit on the bottom branch with his thumb in his mouth. "See me?"

Tom looked at all of them up in the tree. He wished he could join them. Tom couldn't even get up on a branch on the ground, which had fallen down in a storm, and stay on it without falling. "What's the matter with me?" he kept asking himself.

Barnes said, "Hey, I found a nest up here; just look." Tom stretched out and up as far as he could. He couldn't see. "It has three baby birds. Aren't they cute?"

Oliver said, "I go pretty high, don't I, but I get my feet stuck sometimes. Then I turn upside down like a monkey."

Barnes laughed, "You are a monkey."

Allan looked at Tom from the bottom branch and took his thumb out of his mouth long enough to point at Tom and say, "You dummy doodle."

Tom decided he would climb a tree and show them all that he could. He would get to the very top and look down at them. He would sit on the very tippy-top so there wouldn't be any room for Barnes to sit there. He would look down on Oliver in the middle and say, "I'm higher than you are." He would look way down at Allan on the bottom branch and say, "You're yucky."

Well, Tom went home and climbed trees in his dreams all night— red trees, blue trees, yellow trees, purple trees, and, best of all, green trees.

The next morning, he woke up and, to his amazement, there was a new enormous tree standing outside the front door of his house. "It must have grown overnight, just to have me climb it today," he thought. "How nice. Now where shall I start? Trunks all go up, so it doesn't matter. Eeeny, meeny, miny, mo." He took the one in front of him. It was the most obvious. He started to pull himself up. This was a special climbing tree. He could hold onto the bark. It had fur he could hold onto. He began to climb. He pulled himself up with his

front paws. He kept himself from falling down by holding on with his back paws. He climbed all the way to a convenient crotch where he could sit and rest. It was soft and warm. Tom looked down on the pond and his house. He looked all the way over to the farm. He looked down the hill at the trees Barnes and Oliver climbed and they looked tiny. Then something funny happened. A small branch brushed beside him. He held onto it and swung himself up to a higher branch where Tom sat very comfortably. Why hadn't he ever done this before? It was easy.

"My, this is the very best climbing tree I ever climbed. I won't tell Barnes and Oliver about it." Tom looked up. There was one enormous branch left to climb, only one and then Tom would be on top. He wouldn't just be on top of an enormous tree; he would be on top of the world! This branch was very easy to climb. Although it went straight up, it had hair growing all the way up the closest side to him. All that Tom had to do was pull himself up.

"It's easy, my gosh," said Tom. "I'm at the top and there are two handles up here I can hold onto so I won't fall off." He sat there holding onto the handles and looked down. He saw Barnes, Oliver, and Allan walking up the road toward him.

"Hi, down there," he screamed. "Ha, ha, look at me. I did it. I climbed a tree, bigger than you ever saw. I knew I could!"

Barnes, Oliver, and Allan screamed up at him. They had to scream up and up and up, but Tom was so high, he could not even hear them. They screamed and screamed. Finally, he heard them.

"Hey, Tom, what are you doing on top of that giraffe?"

Tom was mad. He hadn't climbed a tree at all.

Tom Turtle
and the Hats

Oliver put on his yellow hard hat and went out into the "construction site," the big sandpile, with bulldozers, backhoes, and pickups, to do some construction work with his trucks.

Oliver put on his policeman's hat, took out his gun and went out to capture bank robbers on his tricycle police car. He talked into his walkie-talkie hand. "Roger, backup unit." Allan followed behind.

Oliver put on his cowboy hat. "Come on, little doggie." He had hold of "Friendy," the cocker spaniel. Oliver rustled cows. "I'm Mac." He herded on the range lawn. "Yuppy-tae-ah-oh."

Oliver put on his fire hat. "Fire! Fire!"

"OK, Johnny." Allan put on his fire hat. They went spray, spray. They put the fires out and hung their red fire hats up on the hooks.

Oliver put on his baseball cap. "Let's play ball." Out they went. They all had baseball caps.

When Oliver couldn't find his hats, he went crazy. He jumped up and down. He couldn't be a policeman if he lost his police hat, or a cowboy if that hat was gone, or a baseball player, or a fireman, or anything. But when he found his hats, he could be anything he wanted to be, and he was all of them.

"I wish I had some hats," said Tom.

"Well, they wouldn't fit; they're too big," said Oliver.

"I still wish I had some hats," said Tom.

Barnes looked at him. "I'll make you some. I'll get acorn hats and paint them different colors." Tom got excited. "This red one's a fire hat; see? This blue one's your baseball cap. This yellow one's a construction hat, and the brown one, well—we don't even have to paint it; it's already brown—that's your cowboy hat. Now you can do anything Oliver does. Just put on the right hat. We'll hang them up here." Barnes molded a block of clay and inserted toothpicks. "That's your hat rack and you'll never lose them, like Oliver always does. Just put 'em back here." Tom was so proud.

"Hey, look at Tom's new hats, boys."

Oliver and Allan looked unimpressed. "Hi, Mr. Acorn Head."

"I got all your hats," said Tom. "See?"

"No, you don't; we got our hats, Mr. Acorn Head."

Barnes shouted at them, "He's got pretend hats. I made them. I painted them; they're pretty."

Tom put all his hats on the toothpick rack. They were pretty—red, yellow, blue, and brown. He left them all on the rack, so they wouldn't get lost, but he never wore any of them.

"Hey, where's Mr. Acorn Head?" asked Oliver.

"I dunno," said Allan.

"Don't say that!" said Barnes.

At night, if you ever came downstairs after everyone had gone to bed, you'd see Oliver's baseball hat walking across the floor after a ball. You'd see Oliver's blue police hat climbing up a pillow onto the plastic police car. You'd see Oliver's cowboy hat sitting on Friendy, the cocker spaniel. You'd see Oliver's fire hat climbing up on the fire engine. You'd see all the hats walking around the house, and, if you picked them up and looked underneath, you'd see Tom Turtle, with a big grin on his face.

The Runaway
Shadow

Playing shadows was a good game. Barnes chased Oliver's shadow on the ground and stomped on it hard.

"Ouch!" said Oliver.

"Did it really hurt, Oliver?"

"Ouch!"

"Let's get Allan."

Allan was standing, his shadow beside him. They clobbered Allan's shadow. "Don't!" Allan screamed.

When they played that game, Tom hid his shadow under the shade of a tree. Tom's shadow wasn't much. It didn't move fast or have things sticking out of it and waving around.

One cloudy day, after finishing tag and playing ball, Oliver said, "Let's play shadows." But they couldn't find them.

"Oh, Oliver, I forgot. You can't play on dark days. They go away," said Barnes.

"Oh," said Oliver, disappointed.

The next day was a bright sunny blue-skyed day. "It's a good day for shadows," said Barnes.

"Yeah, good, Barnes, let's go." They started to chase each other up and down the lawn, their eyes fastened to the ground.

"Oliver, I'll stomp on you—just wait," said Barnes, running. "Boy, your shadow's quick today. Hey, Oliver, where'd you go?"

"I'm right here."

Barnes looked up off the ground and saw Oliver standing beside her.

"Barnes, it's gone."

Barnes looked back down at the ground. There was her shadow. "Your shadow's gone?" said Barnes in astonishment.

"It's gone."

Tom heard Oliver sniffle and came over. "What's wrong?"

"Oliver's shadow's gone."

Tom looked down at the ground. "Mine isn't." At least he had one. "Let's go check Allan." Allan's shadow sat beside him.

"No more shadows," screamed Oliver. "No more nothing! We can't play that. I can't play with you anymore, Barnes."

"You can have mine, Oliver," said Tom.

Oliver wasn't listening. He was thinking how big he was in the afternoon, when their shadows stretched down the road around the corner.

"We're giants, Barnes. Look!" They made animals with their hands—giraffes and deers—and bit each other. Oliver was always a big biting animal. Even then, Allan chased the man in front of him and could never catch up. On the road Tom's lagged behind. His shadow never got much bigger. It never did anything. But Oliver's shadow was a giant and a mean biting animal. It was important to him.

"No more shadow, no more anything," repeated Oliver.

Barnes was searching all over the sun-baked lawn for Oliver's shadow. "We'll find it! It's got to be here."

Tom looked down at his little shadow, no bigger than a ball. "I wish I'd lost you, instead of Oliver's losing his." Tom looked at his shadow. It was crawling away from him. It crawled up the hill.

Tom wasn't moving though. Tom crawled over to Oliver. "Look, Oliver, I lost mine too. I don't like shadows; do you?"

"No," said Oliver, halfheartedly. Oliver was quiet all afternoon.

It was time to go indoors. Oliver started in without his shadow. He really missed it.

"Hey, look, Oliver! My shadow's crawling back," called Tom. "Look, Oliver, it's holding hands with your shadow! It's bringing it back!"

The shadows parted company. Oliver's shadow, with its head bent, walked unsurely over to Oliver, like a naughty little boy. Oliver fell down on the ground and hugged it.

The next day was sunny and Oliver and Barnes played shadows. The next day was cloudy, but Oliver's shadow came out to play when nobody else's did. After that, Oliver's shadow never left him. Tom would look down at his shadow. It was little. It was slow. It wasn't much, but it was a good shadow.

Tom Turtle
and Little Jack

"Oh, Tom," Barnes said, "I almost forgot."

"What?" asked Tom.

"The Jacks for my wild-flower garden."

"Oh," replied Tom.

"Allan, you get the shovel. Oliver, go get the wheelbarrow, because we're going to pick Jacks. It's fun," Barnes added.

The Jack-in-the-Pulpits weren't like flowers. They were beany people, who lived in green houses with elf-shoe shaped roofs. Some people were light green. Some were green and black striped like zebras. Some were all black. The babies were pale green and very little. Barnes, Oliver, and Allan liked to undo things. They unscrewed lamp fixtures. They took tops off pepper shakers. They wrenched knobs off doors. They pulled handles off drawers. They ripped Jacks out of their houses.

"It's mean," said Tom. "They can't get back in their houses."

Barnes handed Allan a Jack. Allan's fingers tore the roof off in a single pull. Then he grabbed the Jack around the middle and yanked him out.

"Good, Allan," said Barnes. Allan wasn't finished. He took the tiny green Jack baby and broke it in half. He rubbed the two halves between his fingers and shredded them. He wiped his hands off on his pants. It was fun.

"It's awful," said Tom, almost in tears.

They had to go down to the chicken house for more. "Don't rip 'em all up," said Barnes. "I need some with roots for the garden."

In the garden, Barnes sorted the Jacks to plant. Oliver dug deep, deep holes with the jabbing shovel. Allan stretched an earthworm until it pulled apart. Barnes put the Jacks left with roots in the holes.

"There," she said, "all planted."

"Hey, who's crying?" asked Tom.

"Not me," said Oliver.

"I aren't," said Allan.

"Must be Truman up at the house," answered Barnes.

"Everybody, quiet!" insisted Tom. It was a strange noise to have everyone quiet.

"It's far away and somebody very little," said Barnes, listening.

"They hurt," said Oliver.

"I do."

"Who said that?" demanded Oliver.

"I did."

"Who are you?" asked Barnes.

"I'm Little Jack."

"What's wrong?" asked Barnes, looking down at the Jacks.

"I miss my Daddy."

"Which one are you?"

"I'm the littlest."

"Here it is," said Barnes, pulling up Little Jack.

"I want my Daddy."

"He must be down at the chicken house," said Barnes. "We took apart all the ones on the road."

"That was mean," said Tom.

"I didn't do it," said Oliver.

"Truman did," said Allan.

Down at the chicken house, Tom said, "Everyone quiet; I hear someone calling."

"It's Daddy up at the house. I'm going," said Oliver.

Oliver and Allan trudged up the hill to the house.

"It's my Daddy!" shouted Little Jack. "It's Daddy!!"

Barnes looked at Tom. They looked at the big patches of Jacks. "Which one?"

Little Jack was crying, "Daddy, Daddy."

Barnes, on her knees, with Tom crawling beside, pushed through the Jacks. Barnes looked for the biggest and best Jack. She planted Little Jack beside it. The leaf from the big Jack twisted around Little Jack's stem and held him close. They didn't speak another word.

Tom
and the
Wild Pail

Up at the vegetable garden, on a path leading into the woods, was a green pail. It was a bright lime green pail that stood out. It was an obnoxious green that didn't fit into the color of the shrub leaves or tree leaves or grass. It did not belong there. But this was a pail and it might be useful.

When Oliver, Allan, Barnes, and Tom drove up to the garden in the green tractor, the pail always caught Tom's eye. He said to Barnes, "Barnes, why don't you pick it up?"

Barnes, who was watching the vegetables grow and had her net ready to slam down on an alighting butterfly, and so was much too busy, said, "No, I can't." The pail became so upsetting to Tom that one day he was not satisfied with her answer, "No, I can't."

"Why can't you?" he asked.

"I can't!"

"Why can't you?" he asked. "You're always looking for pails. They've either lost their handles or have been chewed up by the dog."

"Tom, I can't. That's a wild pail."

Tom looked at the pail again. Now more than the color bothered him. Tom was afraid of the pail. It was turned over on its side. It looked innocuous. It looked like an ordinary pail—but it wasn't. Tom realized now that this wasn't a pail Barnes just didn't want to pick up, because she didn't want to pick it up, because she was busy doing something else, or because she just didn't want to. No, this was a wild pail. Tom didn't know what wild pails did.

Tom searched out Oliver. Oliver didn't like the garden much. It bored him to look at the vegetables.

"Hey, Oliver?" Tom asked.

"Yeah?"

"Do you have the skip rope? Is it tied in a circle? I mean, is it a lasso?"

"Yeah."

"Well, do you want to catch a wild pail?"

"Sure, let's go."

Allan was standing beside the scarecrow. "Oh, oh, oh," he kept saying.

"What's the matter with him?" asked Tom.

"Oh, nothing important," replied Oliver. "He's feeling sorry for the scarecrow. It lost its hat."

Daddy's old straw hat, the one they had filled with black-eyed Susans, with their bright yellow petals and brown eyes, lay on the ground, rotted by the rain and damp earth. Allan and the scarecrow looked alike, both beaten down with their heads sagging.

"He's all right," assured Oliver. "Let's go catch the pail."

Oliver took out his skip-rope lasso, but Oliver couldn't lasso the pail. The knotted circle was too big.

"Try it again; I know you can do it," said Tom.

Oliver did manage to throw the circle of the rope around the pail, but when he pulled, the lasso slipped right over the pail and came back to him.

"It's too hard; I can't do it. It's a hard pail to catch, Tom. It's really wild."

Barnes, who watched them, got interested. "Well, if you want it, I'll get it for you," she said confidently. She ran over to the pail and climbed into the bushes beside it to lift it out. But the prickers and thorns caught in her pants, and she screamed as she felt the scratches on her legs. "I can't do it; it's too wild."

The wild pail frightened Tom, but it also was a challenge for him. "I'll capture that pail and tame it. I'll take it home." Tom crawled under the thorn bushes and dragged the green pail out by its handle in his mouth. He crawled with it to the pond and put the pail upright beside his house. Tom had captured the wild pail.

Tom put a good collection of eating bugs inside it. When he came out to get his dinner, the pail had dumped over on its side, and all the bugs he had caught escaped. Then Tom filled the pail up with the heaviest rocks he could find. Now what would the pail do? It dumped over in front of his eyes. This pail wasn't a plain pail. It was wild.

From the pond, Tom heard Allan crying, "Scarecrow, wanna new hat—pease." Tom crawled over.

"Well, he can't have my cowboy hat; I havta have it," screamed Oliver.

"Oliver, give it," urged Barnes, "or I'll take it."

"Say, I have a hat for the scarecrow," said Tom.

"Wheere?" asked Allan.

"At my house; it's yours if you'll come get it yourself."

Barnes, Oliver, and Allan rushed over to Tom's house.

"That's a pail, Tom!"

"It'd make a good hat," insisted Tom.

"You're right," agreed Barnes. "It's plastic; it wouldn't rot."

"And there's a headband to keep it on too," observed Oliver. "The handle!"

Allan's whole face brightened up. "I going to carry it." Allan picked up the pail and carried it over to the scarecrow's feet. Barnes climbed up to put it on, while Oliver held the scarecrow steady.

Not a crow dared to fly over the garden, or a hedgehog to weasel through the wire underneath the garden fence, for the scarecrow had a new hat. It was the bright lime green pail Barnes wouldn't pick up, and it was the wild pail.

Tom Turtle
Takes a Rest

Tom, Barnes, Oliver, and Allan played all summer long together. They were friends. When Oliver lost a plastic truck driver out of a truck, he'd ask, "Where's Tom; I need him."

If Barnes did something pretty and especially wanted someone to see it, she'd ask, "Where's Tom. I gotta show him my picture."

Even Allan was aware of Tom's presence. When he was not around, Allan asked, "Where'd nice froggie go?"

Fall was almost over. The beautiful trees had shed their leaves. Jack Frost came by more often and powdered the ground with cold white sand and made it hard. The outdoor world was changing, and, with it, everyone was feeling unhappy, as if something were going to happen and it wouldn't be nice.

Tom came over less and less frequently to play. Barnes, Oliver, Allan, and now Truman, steady on his feet, went searching to the pond for Tom.

"Why don't you come play?" Barnes demanded.

"I'm tired," said Tom as he yawned.

"You've been staying up late, and that's naughty," reprimanded Barnes.

"No, I'm tired all the time," answered Tom.

The last time they came to the pond looking for Tom, they found him asleep outside his front door. Oliver turned Tom over on his back to wake him up, but Tom wouldn't turn back over. Tom looked at them out of his weary eyes.

"I've got to go now."

"Go where?" asked Barnes.

"To the bottom of the pond. To the black mud to sleep."

"Why?"

"Because I have to," replied Tom.

"You mean you're going to—going to," said Barnes, thinking long and hard, "hibernate? You're going to stay at the bottom of the pond all winter long!"

"You mean we can't play anymore, then?" asked Oliver.

"Not for now."

"Froggie go away?" Allan asked, looking disturbed.

"We'll all go; come on," said Oliver, pulling his shirt off.

"We can't, Oliver," said Barnes, remembering. "Only turtles can."

"Will you come back and play with us?" pleaded Oliver.

"In the spring," answered Tom, "but you have to help me now. I'm too tired to get over to the pond. You'll have to put me in."

They each took Tom in their hands and kissed him. Barnes's kiss was soft and gentle. Oliver's kiss was slobbery and warm. Allan didn't kiss. He held Tom tightly in his hand and wouldn't let go.

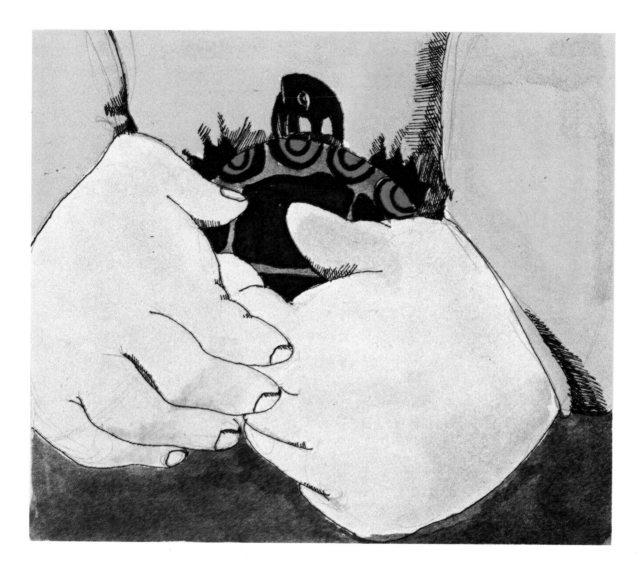

"Throw him in, Oliver," screamed Barnes. "Oliver, pretend he's just a dumb old rock and throw. You have to. Now!"

Oliver grabbed Allan's hand and pulled Tom out. Allan screamed. Like the many rocks they threw into the pond, Oliver threw Tom hard. Tom plummeted into the middle of the pond, and, with the final burst of energy left in him, he plunged like a submarine to the bottom. They all leaned over and watched Tom go to the bottom where it was black, and they couldn't see him anymore.

"Froggie all gone?" asked Allan.

"Oh, Barnes," blurted Oliver. "Oh, Barnes."

"It's all right, Oliver. You'll see. In the spring, we'll find him— as soon as the ice melts, before anyone else does."

Oliver looked down to the black bottom of the pond. He couldn't see anything. The tears blurred his eyes.

"We will, Oliver," said Barnes. "You'll see. Remember your shadow left and it came back. Tom will too. We'll play shadows, pick Jacks and climb trees and go riding and put on hats and catch wild pails. And I won't put any more pussy willows in the house next spring. Tom won't let us do that, will he Oliver?"

"No," said Oliver, sobbing, "and Tom can wear all my hats when he comes back—even my police hat."

"Nice froggie," said Allan.

Barnes took hold of Oliver's arm and pulled. Oliver grabbed Allan's hand and Allan tugged on Truman. They walked up the path to the road. They left the pond behind them. They felt like Tom felt the first day they left him alone outside his beautiful mud-and-stone castle. They felt all alone.

Hand in hand, they walked silently down the road to the farm. But the pony in Barnes wouldn't run. Oliver's trucks stayed on the side of the road untouched. They didn't roar or foam or crash. Allan wasn't complaining; he stayed quiet.

As they walked home, the gray clouds grew dark. They shivered. Out of the sky fell the first flakes of snow. Winter had only begun. Spring was a long time away. They would have to play by themselves, until spring brought them and Tom together again.